It's a Butterfly's Life

Irene Kelly

Holiday House / New York

For Ralph, Kathy, and Katie Coleman
and their magical barn

Library of Congress Cataloging-in-Publication Data
Kelly, Irene.
It's a butterfly's life / by Irene Kelly. — 1st ed.
p. cm.
ISBN-10: 0-8234-1860-X (hardcover)
ISBN-13: 978-0-8234-1860-2 (hardcover)
1. Butterflies—Juvenile literature.
I. Title. QL544.2.K45 2006
595.78'9—dc22
2005046227

The author and publisher
would like to thank Louis N. Sorkin
of the Division of Invertebrate Zoology,
American Museum of Natural History,
for vetting this book
for scientific accuracy.

What is a butterfly's life?

Red Lacewing butterfly

Full of twists and turns . . .

Black Swallowtail caterpillar

Butterflies and moths are insects in the Lepidoptera order. There are about 17,500 different types of butterflies and 160,000 types of moths in the world. Butterflies and moths are a lot alike, but they are not exactly the same.

Buckeye butterfly

Swallowtail butterfly

When a butterfly is resting, it holds its wings straight up or out to its sides.

Spicebush Swallowtail butterfly

Butterflies are out and about during the day. They have thin bodies without much hair and skinny antennae with knobs on the ends.

Most moths come out during the night.

Indian Moon moth

When a moth is resting, it folds its wings into a tent over its body.

They have plump, furry bodies and slim or feathery antennae without knobs on the ends.

Brown China Mark moth

Satin moth

Butterflies have three main body parts: the head, thorax, and abdomen. They have six legs but only use four of them for walking. The feet are important because that's where the butterfly's taste buds are.

You may not be able to taste a cupcake by standing on it, but a butterfly can!

This is a puddle club. The butterflies are sipping minerals and salts out of the mud.

Citrus butterfly

abdomen

antennae

thorax

head

yummy cupcake

A butterfly doesn't have teeth. Instead, it eats by using its proboscis, which is a tongue that works like a straw. Most butterflies feed on nectar from flowers, but some like rotting fruit and tree sap.

As a butterfly drinks from a flower, pollen sticks to its body. When it visits another flower, the pollen falls off, and presto—the plant is

pollinated!

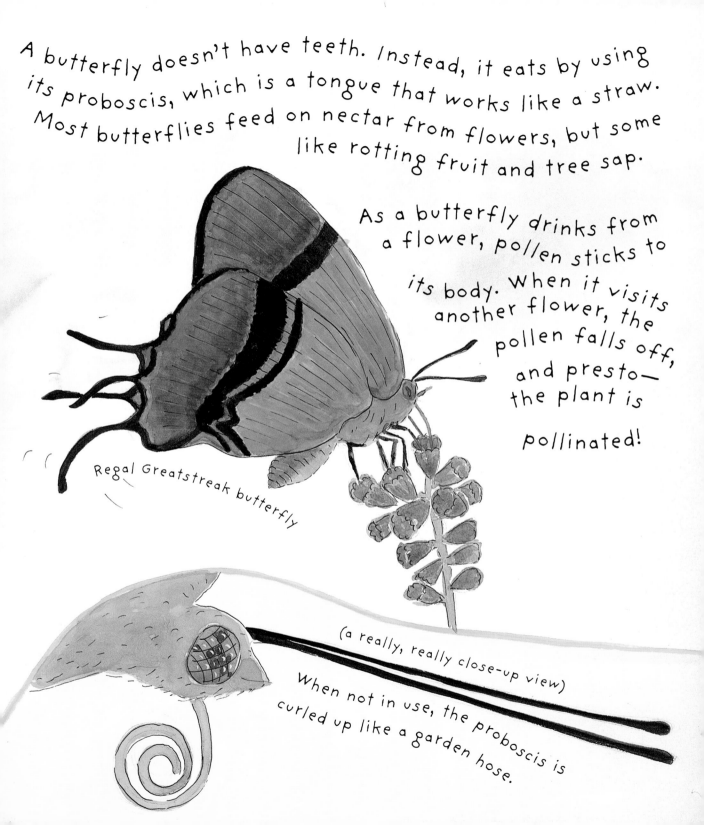

Regal Greatstreak butterfly

(a really, really close-up view)

When not in use, the proboscis is curled up like a garden hose.

Butterflies fly by rippling their wings up and down slowly and gliding on air currents, just like birds. They can fly long distances this way.

If a butterfly is too cold, its muscles won't work and it can't fly. To warm up, butterflies bask in the sun, their wings soaking up the sun's rays like solar panels.

Sometimes butterflies flutter around in crazy patterns to confuse hungry birds. This is called dodging.

Mexican Blue Wing butterfly

A butterfly has four beautiful wings. Each wing has shimmering scales that overlap like shingles on a roof.

Eastern Tiger Swallowtail butterfly

(close-up)

You should never touch a butterfly's wings because the tiny scales will scatter like powder. That could injure the butterfly.

Some butterflies migrate huge distances. The Monarch wins the prize for the longest migration of all. Every fall, millions of Monarchs fly all the way from the midwestern United States to central Mexico. For some, that's a three-thousand-mile trip!

Monarchs don't weigh much. Five Monarchs weigh only as much as one penny.

Migrating Monarchs may fly up to eighty miles in just one day. They stop briefly to rest or feed on nectar.

Some butterflies live their whole lives in one place. They hibernate in sheltered spots when the weather turns cold. A chemical in their blood keeps them from freezing.

The Comma butterfly hibernates among dried leaves.

A butterfly's most important job is to mate and lay eggs.

Giant Swallowtail butterfly

The male swoops and dives, showing off his colorful wings in hopes of catching the eye of a female. He spreads around a special scent that the female likes.

The female picks up the scent with her antennae.

If the male's wings are the shape and pattern the female is looking for, she will mate with him.

Sometimes the male claims an area as his home. He will chase away any other males that come into his territory . . . but he always welcomes females.

Most butterflies only live for a short time, so they must mate and lay eggs quickly.

They join together at the tips of their abdomens, facing opposite directions.

Green-Spotted Triangle butterfly

They might stay together this way for only an hour or up to an entire day. If they're disturbed, they can fly away still attached, with one of them flying backward!

When the mating is over, the male flies away.
The female gets right to work. She flutters around,
tasting plants with her feet. For many species,
only one type of plant will do.

Eventually she finds the perfect
one for her caterpillars to feed
on as soon as they hatch.

Baltimore Checkerspot
butterfly

If you are ever in a forest and smell chocolate,
look around for a Wall Brown butterfly.
The male sends out a chocolaty scent
to attract a female.

From a few days to several weeks after the egg is laid, it is ready to hatch. The caterpillar chomps through the eggshell with its sharp jaws. The caterpillar crawls out of the egg and makes the eggshell its first meal.

The eggs can be smooth or shiny, patterned or ridged.

Vine

Postman butterflies lay just one egg.

Peacock butterflies lay their eggs in piles.

Mourning Cloak butterflies lay their eggs in perfect rows.

A caterpillar is a leaf-eating machine. Just two weeks after hatching, Monarch caterpillars are 2,700 times their original weight!

(close-up)

milkweed leaf

If a newborn baby gained weight that fast, it would weigh eight tons in fourteen days. That's as big as two full-grown rhinos!

Caterpillars must eat fast, since many creatures want to eat them.

Caterpillar droppings are called frass. The frass of a small caterpillar is the size of the period at the end of this sentence. But the frass of a full-grown caterpillar can be as big as an apple seed. When many caterpillars are together in a tree, their falling frass sounds like rain as it hits the ground.

Some caterpillars can "shoot" their frass up to three feet away!

As a caterpillar gets bigger, it outgrows its skin and sheds it. This is called molting. Now the caterpillar has a new skin to grow into. A caterpillar will molt four or five times before it is full grown.

Pipevine Swallowtail caterpillar

American Painted Lady caterpillar

Zebra Swallowtail caterpillar

Swallowtail caterpillars can put out horns that give off a stinky odor when the caterpillars feel threatened.

Spicebush Swallowtail caterpillar horns

(close-up)

Caterpillars move slowly, making them easy targets for predators. They need good camouflage or a scary appearance to survive.

Praying Mantis

Some caterpillars of the Metalmark and Hairstreak butterflies can call for help when they are being attacked. They make vibrating sounds. This noise is their way of yelling, "HELP!"

Guess what comes to their rescue?

Ants! The ants chase away the hungry predators, and the caterpillars reward them by giving off a sweet juice called honeydew.

Ant drinking honeydew

Some caterpillars have eyespots that make them look like snakes.

Others are disguised to look like bird droppings.

Giant Swallowtail caterpillar

Viceroy caterpillar

Spicebush Swallowtail caterpillar

How can a slowpoke caterpillar turn into a fluttering butterfly? This change is called metamorphosis. When a caterpillar is ready, it makes silky threads that it uses to attach itself to a branch or leaf.

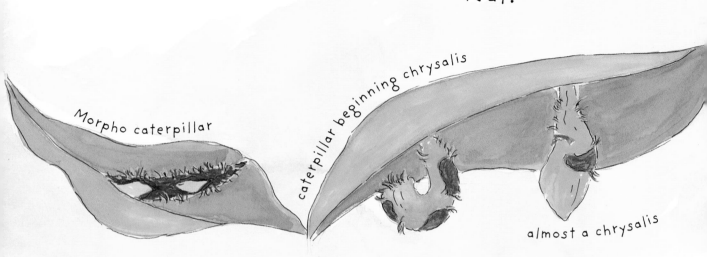

Morpho caterpillar

caterpillar beginning chrysalis

almost a chrysalis

Then the caterpillar's skin splits, revealing the pupa or chrysalis. Like a shield, the outside of the chrysalis protects the caterpillar inside as it changes into a butterfly.

becoming a Morpho pupa

finished Morpho pupa

Inside the chrysalis the caterpillar's body breaks down. A butterfly's head, body, and wings take shape.

Queen Page Swallowtail chrysalis

Common Bluebottle chrysalis

Owl butterfly chrysalis

Each type of caterpillar has its own special chrysalis. Some are camouflaged to look like bird droppings, leaves, or twigs. A few look like sparkling jewels.

Monarch chrysalis

1 swallowtail chrysalis

2

In all that time, only one drop of waste has accumulated.

Just before the butterfly is ready to come out, the chrysalis becomes see-through. Then the chrysalis cracks and the insect swallows air to plump up.

The new butterfly pushes out with its legs. Its wings are squished together. Before it can fly, it must uncrinkle them.

③

④

The insect hangs upside down and unfurls its wings, and its veins fill with fluid. More than an hour later, the wings have hardened.

swallowtail

butterfly

The butterfly flutters its wings a few times and flies away . . .

in search of a mate.

The Brimstone butterfly is well hidden when it is resting in a tree.

When the Hoary Comma butterfly closes its wings, the butterfly is camouflaged.

But when it is disturbed, its wings open . . .

The Glasswing butterfly is hard to spot because its wings are see-through.

startling any predator with a burst of color.

Some butterflies have gigantic spots on their wings that look like eyes.

Peacock butterfly

These false eyes fool hungry predators into thinking that the butterfly is much bigger and fiercer than it really is.

The leaf pattern on this butterfly's wings helps the insect hide.

Rajah Brooke's Birdwing butterfly

Bats and birds love to eat butterflies and moths, but people are a bigger threat. When forests are destroyed for logging or to make way for buildings, butterfly and moth habitats are also destroyed.

Zebra
Swallowtail
endangered

Philippine
Swallowtail
endangered

Xerces
EXTINCT

Large Copper
EXTINCT

Water pollution and air pollution are also dangerous to butterflies. Many species have disappeared forever while others are seriously endangered.

endangered

The Queen Alexandra's Birdwing is endangered because its rain forest home is being destroyed. It is the biggest butterfly in the world, with a wingspan of one foot. That's as big as a cardinal's wingspan! This giant butterfly lives in Papua, New Guinea.

Want to see butterflies up close? If you plant their favorite flowers, they will stop by for a sip!

Here are a few plants that lots of butterflies and caterpillars like.

butterfly bush

purple coneflowers

lilacs

snapdragons

daisies

You can plant a garden in your yard or in a pot. Find a sunny place so your visitors can enjoy a sunbath . . .

. . . and don't forget a muddy spot for puddling!

sunflowers

bee balm

zinnias

impatiens

AMING BUT TRUE

Lycaenid pupa hissing and shaking

Most chrysalises are still and silent, making them fast food for many predators. But some can hiss. Others squeak and shake to frighten their enemies.

Caterpillars have several thousand muscles, while you and I have about five hundred.

Cabbage butterfly caterpillar

Some caterpillars can survive underwater for hours.

Caterpillars have twelve very simple eyes, but they can't see well out of any of them.

simple eyes

Spicebush Swallowtail caterpillar